D0033782

EVERY CRIME SOLVED!

Jack McGurk is the president of the McGurk Detective Agency, the agency that handles—and solves—every mystery it tackles. Who would ever guess that McGurk and his partners are no older than ten? Can you match wits with McGurk and his friends? Try this mystery and see!

A McGURK MYSTERY #2

The Case of the Condemned Cat

by E.W. Hildick
Illustrated by Lisl Weil

AN ARCHWAY PAPERBACK
POCKET BOOKS · NEW YORK

POCKET BOOKS, a Simon & Schuster division of
GULF & WESTERN CORPORATION
1230 Avenue of the Americas, New York, N.Y. 10020

Published by arrangement with Macmillan Publishing Co., Inc.
Library of Congress Catalog Card Number: 75-14196

ISBN: 0-671-29888-7

First Pocket Books printing August, 1978

10 9 8 7 6 5 4 3

Trademarks registered in the United States and other countries.

Printed in the U.S.A.

Contents

1

Murder!

Murder. That was the sort of mystery the McGurk Organization had to investigate this time. A real killing. And a client who had been accused of it. A client under sentence of death. A client whose name we just had to clear.

1

The case came to us early one Saturday morning. McGurk had called a special meeting. A "training session" is what he called it.

"It's been a few weeks since we had a real investigation," he said. "You know. Looking for clues. Working out what they mean."

"So?" I said.

"So we're becoming rusty. Out of practice."

"So?" said Wanda Grieg.

She has known McGurk as long as I have. She is just as suspicious of him when he has a certain gleam in his eyes. They had that gleam in them now.

"So we have a training session," said McGurk, running a hand through his bright red hair, trying to smooth it down. (Another suspicious sign.) "We all go into the yard and hunt around. We gather up things that people have dropped. Then we try to work out who dropped them—what sort of people, and why."

"Hey! That sounds like a good idea!" said Willie Sandowsky.

He hasn't lived around here for long. He

still has a lot to learn about McGurk. But I must admit it sounded like a good idea to Wanda and me, too. So we went into McGurk's yard and we started picking up "clues."

Ha! "Clues"!

Three pailsful of them. All inside a half-hour. Things like cigarette butts, candy wrappers, broken combs, rusty nails, screws. Well, *two and a half* pailsful, because Willie was slower than Wanda and me. He had to keep sniffing at his "clues" with that long nose of his. He claims that it's as sensitive as it is long. McGurk and Wanda believe him. I'm still not sure.

Anyway, the real point is not Willie's nose. The real point is that we three were the pail carriers. Wanda, Willie, and I did all the bending and picking up, while McGurk just strolled around directing operations.

"There's more here," he kept saying. "You've missed some over here. And here . . . ."

Well, fair enough. If this was a training session for the McGurk Organization, McGurk himself had every right to lead it.

But we thought differently at the end of the half-hour. I mean when Mrs. McGurk came out and said to him:

"Well, I must say it's looking a lot tidier now. You're very lucky, Jack, having such good friends to help you with your chores."

So *that* was it!

"Chores!" said Wanda, when Mrs. McGurk had gone. "I oughta empty this pail over your head!"

"Me, too!" said Willie.

"A clear case of fraud!" I said. "A rotten con trick!"

"Now listen, men," said McGurk, backing away as we advanced with our pails of litter. "We can still examine them for clues. It's still good training. It's—"

"Hey, McGurk! Joey! Willie! Wanda! I— I need your help. Real bad!"

It was Ray Williams. He'd come running up to us. He's usually a very quiet kid. And being a year older than any of us—nearly twelve—he doesn't usually take too much notice of us. So right away he made us forget our argument and turn and stare at him. Then we saw how pale he was and we stared harder.

"What's wrong, Ray?" said McGurk. "You look—"

"You still running your detective organization?" said Ray.

He pointed to the notice on the door leading from the yard into McGurk's basement:

HEADQUARTERS
KEEP OUT

THE McGURK
ORGANIZATION
✳✳✳✳
PRIVATE INVESTIGATIONS
MYSTERIES SOLVED
PERSONS PROTECTED

"Yes," said McGurk. "Sure. Why?"

"Because I have a case for you," said Ray. "An urgent one. A matter of life and death."

"It sounds like murder," I said, half joking.

"It *is!*" said Ray.

"You'd better come into the office," said McGurk, leading the way down the four steps to the basement door.

2
The Victim

Ray Williams wasn't very interested in our office. He was much more concerned about the crime. But he sat down where McGurk told him to: on a chair in front of the long table we use as a desk, facing McGurk.

McGurk sat in the old rocking chair, as usual. I sat at one of the narrow ends of the table, my notebook and pencil ready. Wanda and Willie just stood around, listening.

"Right," said McGurk, rocking back and nodding at Ray. "First things first. Who's the victim of this murder?"

"Well," said Ray, "in a way the real victim is Whiskers. But I suppose the *actual* victim is one of the Overshaws' doves. You know— one of those two white pigeons."

McGurk scowled at him. So did I. He'd already caused me to muddle up my first entry in the notebook.

"Who's Whiskers?" I said.

"Never mind that!" snapped McGurk. "Who's *dead?*"

"Well, the dove," said Ray. "One of—"

"O.K.!" said McGurk. He jabbed a finger at my notebook. "Get that down: 'Victim, a dove.'"

"Isn't Whiskers that stray cat you took in?" asked Wanda sympathetically.

"Yes," said Ray. "He—"

"Officer Grieg!" yelled McGurk. "Kindly

keep quiet. *I* do the questioning here. . . . Now then," he said, turning to Ray. "Next question. Scene of the crime?"

"Well, our back yard. Far end. That's why Whiskers is being blamed. He—"

"When did the murder take place?"

"This morning sometime. I—"

"You don't know for sure?"

"No. They all figure it must have happened a few hours ago. Before breakfast. Nobody saw it happen, but—"

"Ah!" cried McGurk. "No witnesses, eh?"

"Well, no. It was—"

"So how come this Whiskers gets the blame?"

"Well," said Ray, shrugging and looking very unhappy, "that's just it. Just because he's a cat. Just because the feathers were all over our back lawn. Just because he was sniffing around them."

I looked up.

"That's what they call circumstantial evidence," I said, glad of the chance to use a real police-type word.

"Yes," said McGurk—as if he knew. "That's what that's called. It looks bad for

the cat. Very bad. What makes you so sure he *didn't* do it?"

"Cats do chase pigeons," said Wanda, still very sympathetic, but shaking her head sadly.

"Not Whiskers!" said Ray. "And anyway, even if cats do chase pigeons, they rarely catch them. They very rarely mean anything when they chase birds that big. Even blue jays. And Whiskers doesn't even go after *sparrows.*"

"Tell us more about the victim," said Mc-Gurk, frowning at the rest of us to be quiet. "Did you say it was one of those two white doves the Overshaws keep?"

"Yes."

"Then really it's Mr. and Mrs. Overshaw who should be coming to us," said McGurk. "If they want to solve the mystery."

"That's just *it!*" said Ray, beginning to look annoyed with McGurk. "Didn't you hear what I said? *They* don't think there's any mystery. They think it was Whiskers."

"They're pretty mad about it, are they?"

"Well, no. Not really. More sad. Mrs. Overshaw said it was only natural, too. Everybody says that. But they're wrong. Wrong

13

where Whiskers is concerned, anyway. I know."

"All right," said McGurk. "I believe you. But what's the difference? If they're not mad, why worry?"

"Why worry?" howled Ray. "When they're going to have Whiskers put to sleep for it? *You'd* worry if—"

"Who?" said McGurk. "Who's having him put to sleep? Why?"

"My parents, that's who. They're scared stiff of having trouble with the neighbors, that's why. And besides, they never really did want me to keep him in the first place. It's an excuse."

Wanda looked as if she was going to cry in sympathy.

"Have they said? Have they actually *said?*" she asked.

"They've said practically the same thing," said Ray. "Whiskers is going to be taken to the pound this afternoon."

"Hm!" McGurk was rocking slowly, his eyes half closed. "I like that, I like that."

"What?" roared Ray, getting up and leaning forward.

"Cool it!" said McGurk. "I only mean I like that sort of case. Where somebody is wrongly accused of murder and the detective has to prove him innocent. Save his life."

"Yes, well," murmured Ray. "Like I say. There isn't much time in *this* case. You'll take it, then?"

For an answer, McGurk turned to me.

"Got it all down so far?"

I pushed my notebook across.

He glanced at it. Here is the page:

Nature of crime: MURDER
Victim: ~~This~~ One of Overshaws' doves
Murderer: ?
Client: Whiskers (Ray Williamses' cat)
Wrongfully accused?

"Right," said McGurk. "We'll take it. It looks easy enough to me."

"Easy?" gasped Willie, who was probably still wondering who the Overshaws were.

"Yes," said McGurk. "All we have to do is fill in that blank space." He tapped the notebook. "Find out who the real murderer was. Then they'll have to let our client off."

He stood up.

"And since time's running short, men," he said, "let's not waste any more of it. Let's go and investigate the scene of the crime. Talk to the other neighbors. Find out if anybody heard anything, saw anything."

On the way out, I had a quiet word with McGurk.

"Suppose we find a clue that says it *is* Whiskers, though?"

"Well, at least Ray will know for sure," he said. "The cat won't be condemned just on—er—circle special evidence."

"The word is 'circumstantial,' " I corrected him.

"That's what I said," replied McGurk.

3

The Scene of the Crime

On the way over to Ray's yard, we were all fairly quiet. I mean we felt sorry for Ray, yes. But we were also doubtful about saving Whiskers. I was, anyway.

Even McGurk was quiet.

But once we reached the scene of the crime he began to brighten up.

"Well!" he kept murmuring, as he walked around the Williamses' lawn. "Now how about *that?* . . . Hmm! . . . No. Keep back. Don't tramp all over the evidence, *please!*"

At first I thought he was bluffing. After all, it was not as if there were any fragile clues. You know, clues that might get tromped into the earth or broken. It wasn't even as if there was a body—lying in a certain position, the way they lie on TV so that the police can paint a white line around them and work out what happened in the death struggle.

There weren't any ordinary clues at all. No cigarette butts, no match sticks, no broken combs, no empty cartridges, etc. The Williamses' back yard was mostly grass, kept nice and short and smooth and very neat. The opposite of McGurk's. We wouldn't have been able to collect enough ordinary litter to fill a thimble, never mind a pail.

No, the only clues were the feathers. Dozens. Scores. White feathers. Big ones, small ones, some just bits of fluff really. All over the far end of the yard.

And nothing else.

No claws, no beak, no bones.

"It must have been hungry," said Willie.

Ray scowled.

"*What* must?"

"Well, the cat."

Ray scowled harder.

"*Which* cat?"

"Er—well—whichever cat did it."

"Huh!" grunted Ray. "Weren't you listening at *all*?"

But McGurk was pleased with Willie's remark.

"Good thinking, Willie. I was just going to say the same. Whatever killed that bird must have been hungry. . . . But—hey!—stand back. You're disturbing the evidence."

Willie nearly fell over in his hurry to get back away from the feathers.

Wanda's lip curled. She'd been made to jump, too.

"Disturbing it? How in the heck can any-one disturb that mess? Look, the *breeze* is moving some of them, anyway."

"I know," said McGurk. "But there *is* a pattern. Joey"—he turned to me—"stand on this roller and look down. Then draw a plan in your notebook and mark where the feathers are thickest. . . . Go on. Just pencil dots will do."

"But what good will it be?" I said.

It didn't seem much use to me. But it *looked* efficient, I guess. And it did help to give Ray a bit of confidence.

"Yeah!" he growled. "Do as McGurk says!"

"Oh, all right!" I said.

"And show the yards on either side," said McGurk. "Including the Overshaws'. Only don't bother with *their* details. Just this one."

So I balanced on the roller and drew my rough plan while the others stood around. And you know what? As soon as I started really looking I could see there *was* a bit of a pattern to those feathers.

Here is the plan, which I copied out later on plain white paper:

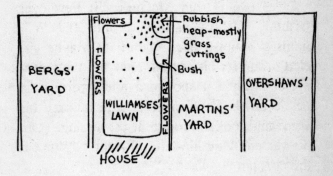

The dots are to show where the feathers were more concentrated and where they were more scattered.

When I had finished, McGurk looked over my shoulder and nodded wisely.

"Yes. That's good. That is an important record."

"Of *what?*"

Wanda's lip was curled again.

"Of the victim's last few moments."

McGurk said it in such a way that Wanda's lip uncurled and her mouth fell open and we became quiet.

"Go on!" whispered Willie.

"Yes, well," said McGurk. "It flew over Gramp Martin's yard and onto the Williamses' rubbish heap, didn't it? Maybe circled around a bit at first, enjoying the morning sun. Then it spotted a juicy worm or a beetle on the rubbish heap." He lowered his voice and looked around at us, leering. (Oh, he was enjoying himself, all right!) "What it did *not* spot . . . was . . ."

"Go on!"

"The killer. Lurking. Lurking under the bush."

"You mean a cat after all?" I said.

"I tell you Whiskers wouldn't ever do that!" cried Ray.

"Who said anything about Whiskers?" said McGurk. "In fact, the more I look at the evidence, the more I am sure that an ordinary cat—a pet sort of cat—*couldn't* have done it."

"Well, Whiskers *was* a stray, you know," I said.

"You shut up!" shouted Ray. "I tell you—"

"We're wasting time," said McGurk. "And the next important step is to interview the client. Where is Whiskers?"

"In the house. My mother says he's got to stay there until—until—"

"Under house arrest, eh?" said McGurk. "Fair enough. But do you think she'd mind if we went in to have a word with him? I mean —to take a *look* at him?"

"She better not!" growled Ray. "It's the least she can do!"

4

Whiskers

I'd never really studied Mrs. Williams before. But when she came to the door that morning I could see what Ray was up against. She was a small dark woman, with a very quiet, quick sort of voice, as nervous as a cat herself. Just the sort to be scared of what the neighbors might think.

Yet she seemed as though she could be stubborn.

She didn't mind us all going into the kitchen to see Whiskers, no.

"So long as you keep your voices down. Your father's trying to get some sleep, you know," she said to Ray. "He works on the night shift," she explained to the rest of us.

Then to everyone:

"But don't think it will do any good!"

As I said: stubborn. With stubborn wrinkles all around her little mouth when she'd finished speaking and had closed it tight.

"Don't think *what* will do any good?" demanded Ray.

"You know very well! Getting your friends to sympathize is what I mean. I sympathize too, you know. Don't think I don't. But we just can*not* keep a cat that will cause trouble with the neighbors."

More stubborn wrinkles.

Then she left us with our client.

As for *him* . . .

Nervous as a *cat*, did I say?

Well, if there was one thing this cat wasn't, it was nervous.

All the time the woman who was going to have him put to sleep was talking, he'd sat there on a high stool squeezing his eyes and looking pleased. I mean you'd have thought she'd been *praising* him. There he'd sat, paws folded in front like the Sphinx, and all the fur around his neck puffed out like a ruff. Really *placid*.

Then, when Mrs. Williams left, he slowly unfolded himself, stood up, arched his back, lifted his bottom, blinked, yawned, gave a little chirp, and jumped down to meet us.

He was a tabby cat. Gray, with black stripes and a white chin. Clear green eyes and a pink nose. And a mouth edged with black so that when he turned his head you could see at once that he was wearing a happy smile.

The first one he went up to—tail in the air with a hook on the end of it, like a question mark—was Wanda.

"What a lovely cat!" she said, as it rubbed against her legs.

Then it moved on.

"Doesn't look like a killer cat to me!" said Willie, as it rubbed against his legs.

"Me, either," I said, when it kissed me.

Well, it did! I was bending down to get a better look at its chin for my notebook description, when—plunk!—it stuck out its pink nose to meet my nose and gave it a cold wet dab.

"*Now* do you see what I mean?" said Ray, looking around at us.

Wanda, Willie, and I nodded. Firmly.

Only McGurk wasn't saying anything. Not even when it butted its head softly against his right shin and burst out purring.

"Well?" said Ray, glaring at McGurk.

McGurk looked up.

"What's his regular food?" was all he said.

Ray looked angrier than ever.

"What d'you mean—regular? You trying to—?"

"What do you usually give him to eat?" said McGurk, blinking as placidly as the cat.

"Huh! I don't see—"

"Just tell me. It's important."

"Well—this."

31

Ray reached up to a shelf and pulled down a can of cat food.

The cat's purring grew even louder. It leaped back onto the stool and sat up squeezing.its eyes at Ray——gleaming green slits.

McGurk's eyes were doing a bit of gleaming, too.

"When?" he asked softly.

"Huh? When what?"

"When does he usually get fed?"

"Oh——well——early evening."

"No other time?"

"No. That's what the cat book said. I——"

"Right!" said McGurk. "Give him some now."

"But it's not time. It——oh——you think he——it——"

"Just try him with some now."

Ray was already opening the can. Whiskers was already off the stool, rubbing away at Ray's legs.

"There!" said Ray, putting down the saucer.

"Yuff!" said Whiskers, as his pink nose dug into the meat.

"He's enjoying it anyway," said Wanda.

"Yeah," sighed Willie. "He seems to know it's his last—"

I nudged him to be quiet.

We were probably all thinking the same thing anyway.

All except McGurk.

He was nodding—nodding and grinning.

"O.K., Whiskers," he said, as the cat went on gobbling. "I believe you. You're innocent. We'll clear your name. We—"

He stopped and looked up as Mrs. Williams came into the kitchen.

"I'm just going to the supermarket, Raymond. So remember what I said. No noise. And close the door quietly when you go out."

"Ma'am," said McGurk, in his best police-inspector manner. "Before you go I'd like you to know that you've been making a terrible mistake. This cat is innocent and we intend to—"

"It's no use, little boy," said Mrs. Williams, not meaning to insult McGurk but doing it. "It was found with the feathers—some of them still warm—and that is that."

"But, ma'am," said McGurk, "it's just eaten a whole saucer of cat food. If it had eaten the dove—bones and all, don't forget—it wouldn't have wanted another meal so soon."

"No, Mom!" said Ray, suddenly looking hopeful.

"It would have been sleeping it off," said Wanda.

"Yeah!" said Willie. "Like the lions at the zoo!"

"I agree," I said.

But it was no use. She was shaking her head.

"I'm sorry," she said. "I really am. But he was caught in the act. Practically. And as soon as your father gets up this afternoon he's taking it to the pound. They—they won't be cruel."

"Ha!" grunted Wanda. "Putting it to sleep's not *my* idea of—"

"Now then, little girl. It may not even come to that. They—they might find a good home for it. You never know."

Then Mrs. Williams left, quickly, before anyone else gave her an argument—just as timid as she was stubborn. What a mixture!

"Impossible!" said Ray. "Didn't I warn you? She won't listen. She *wants* the cat out of the way."

"She's not the only one," murmured Mc-Gurk.

"And what do you mean by that?" said Ray.

"No . . . nothing. . . . Anyway, from what she says she isn't exactly dying to have it put to sleep, is she?"

"No," grumbled Ray. "But that's what *will* happen. The ASPCA gets so many stray cats. They couldn't possibly—"

"What I'm getting at," said McGurk, "is this. If you opened the door now and the cat ran away, your mother wouldn't mind. Would she? Just so long as it didn't go on living *here.*"

"Yes. Sure. But he just won't run away. You think I haven't *tried* opening the door?"

McGurk shrugged.

"Well, try again. Only this time we'll give him some help. Have you an old tote bag? One with a zipper?"

Ray looked doubtful.

"*We* have," said Wanda.

"Go and get it then," said McGurk. "Quick. . . . Now—let me think . . . Oh, yes! Willie, *your* father and mother don't do much gardening, do they?"

Willie grinned shyly. The Sandowskys' yard was even worse than McGurk's.

"No. Why?"

"I mean they don't use that shed at the back of the yard much."

"No. Not at all."

"Good!" said McGurk, stooping to give our client a quick scratch between the ears. "So as soon as Officer Grieg gets back, we'll whisk old Whiskers into the bag and smuggle him into Willie's shed."

"What?" cried Ray.

"Shush! You'll wake your dad," warned McGurk. Then: "Yes. About the shed. Why not? That's the first thing a good Detective Organization does in a case like this. Isn't it?"

We stared. The others were still not quite with him—though I was beginning to see.

"Yes," I said. "We have to—"

"We have to get the client to a place of safety while we investigate," said McGurk. He looked down. "Haven't we, sir?"

"Brrr-up!" agreed Whiskers.

5

Journey to Safety

Whiskers was still cheerful when Wanda put the bag down in front of him.

It was a large airline bag with the letters TWA on it.

"Heh! heh!" cackled McGurk, as the cat sniffed around the opening.

41

"What's so funny *now?*" said Ray.

"Those initials. They fit."

"Fit?"

"Yes. Take Whiskers Away. Heh! heh!"

McGurk cackled again. The rest of the Organization groaned. Ray growled.

"This is no joke, McGurk. This—"

"Ooh! Look!" gasped Wanda. "He's getting in by himself."

She was right. All we could see of Whiskers was his back end rearing out of the opening, with his tail swishing slowly.

"He knows what's good for him," said Mc-Gurk.

But of course Whiskers was only curious. As Ray gently pressed his backside and tail farther in, and McGurk closed the zipper to within an inch of the end, that cat stopped being cheerful. He became alarmed instead and started bumping about inside and scratching.

And when Ray picked up the bag and said, "Let's go then," that cat stopped being alarmed and became angry.

"Nyah! Nyah!" it started yelling, in a very peevish tone.

And then, when we went walking out of the house and yard and down the street, that cat stopped being angry and became very sorry for itself.

"Woe! Woe!" it kept crying, particularly when we went around corners. "Woe!"

It sounded more like "Waw!"—but it was "Woe!" all right. There was no mistaking the tone.

"Poor thing!" said Wanda. "He seems to know he's being taken farther and farther away from home."

Willie bent down to the bag and said:

"If you knew what was good for you, you'd be whistling for joy, kid!"

"Woe! woe!" moaned Whiskers, louder than ever.

"Shut up, both of you!" said McGurk to Willie and the bag. "We don't want your mother and father to think we're taking something alive into the shed."

We were at the Sandowskys' front gate, next door to ours.

"That's all right," said Willie. "They're out shopping."

"Good," said McGurk. "So let's get it over

43

with. But—hey!—wait. . . . Just in case Joey's mother glances over this way, let's walk down the yard *casually*. Right? Ray— swing the bag about as if there was just some books in it. Or football gear. You others— stop *looking* at it."

Ray had been carrying the bag stiff-armed, trying to give Whiskers as smooth and steady a ride as possible. But he must have seen some sense in McGurk's suggestion. He began to swing it about.

Then Whiskers set up the loudest moan yet.

"Woe! Oh woe! Oh woe! woe! woe!" he cried, all the way to the shed.

The shed was an old one—good and strong, but old, with flaking green paint and dirty windows. The door creaked like something out of a horror movie when Willie opened it. Rust fluttered off the hinges. Cobwebs tickled our faces.

"It's nice and dark in here, anyway," said Wanda.

"Yes," said McGurk. "I knew it would be a good spot. Too bad there's no key, though."

45

"That's all right," said Willie. "It's a nice stiff catch. He won't break out."

"I was thinking of people coming *in,* you dum-dum!"

"Well, like I said. No one ever comes in here—not even me. Much."

My eyes were getting used to the dimness.

"We can fill this old seed box with soil for its litter box. And these old sacks should make a nice bed."

"Are they dry?" asked Ray.

46

They were. What was more, they were on a wide shelf about waist-high, at the far end of the shed.

"Well away from the door," I said. "No drafts."

"He could hide out in here for a month," said Willie.

"That won't be necessary," said McGurk.

"There's certainly plenty of old junk for him to investigate," said Wanda.

And the cat? What did Whiskers himself say during those first few minutes?

Nothing.

The bag was silent.

"O.K.," said McGurk. "The door's tight shut. You can let him out."

"Well, stand back, then," said Ray.

Then he bent down to the zipper and said softly:

"Now it's all right, Whiskers. It won't be for long. It's a dirty, lousy, crummy hole, I know—"

"Huh!" snorted Willie, and with *his* nose he can really snort.

"—but you'll be safe here," continued Ray. "So—easy, boy—out you come."

For a few seconds, there was no movement. We thought the cat was either sulking or making up its mind which of us to spring at first.

Then, gradually, in the dimness, up loomed its head, looking bigger and rounder than ever, ears cocked forward, eyes glinting. Then out came one front paw, slowly. Then the other. Then—with a soft plonk!—the whole body.

And now he kept his head down, whiskers twitching, nose to the floor, sniffing as he went forward step by step.

Then:

"Hey! He's *purring!*" said Willie. "He *likes* it here!"

"The lamb!" murmured Wanda.

"Thank goodness for that!" sighed Ray.

I was going to add something about what a spunky and almost *human* animal Whiskers seemed, but McGurk cut it short.

"Right, men!" he said. "Now we've got the client safely stashed away, let's get on with *our* investigation."

6

Strange Noises

The first thing we did after that was interview the neighbors.

Naturally, we decided to start with the next-door neighbors. And just as naturally, we decided to go first to Mrs. Berg. That's because she isn't a bad sort. Gramp Martin, on the other hand, is a regular old grouch, always grumbling about kids going into his yard for balls and things. He still hadn't gotten over the time we chased a prime suspect into his yard when we were investigating the Mystery of the Missing Glove.

"So we'll try Mrs. Berg first," said McGurk. "Who knows? She might come up with a clue that will solve the whole thing right away."

Well, Mrs. Berg didn't seem as though she'd give us any sort of clues at first. Then again, it took her a few minutes to get over the sight of the five of us all crowded on her doorstep, staring up.

As I say, she isn't a bad sort. She doesn't *mind* kids. I mean, how can she, when she had six of her own, now all grown up? But she's the rather fat, flustery type. And I suppose we did look a bit menacing—four of us holding up ID cards and the fifth looking ready to burst into tears.

"What—oh, dear—has something happened?"

"Yes, ma'am," said McGurk. "A murder."

Well, that didn't help to calm her any.

She gave a little yell, then put a hand to her mouth.

"That—that isn't a nice thing to joke about, Jack McGurk."

"I know, ma'am."

"You're telling me!" said Ray.

"But it's true," said Wanda.

"Even if it *is* only a dove," said Willie.

"Oh!" Mrs. Berg looked relieved. "That!"

"You know about it then, ma'am?"

McGurk's eyes glittered so hard that she became flustered again.

"Well, yes. The feathers, yes. . . . I thought, what a shame. One of the Overshaws' birds, wasn't it? I like doves. Lovely birds, doves. It was probably a cat, I suppose."

"It wasn't either," Ray blurted out. "At least it wasn't *our*—"

"Leave the investigating to us," said McGurk. He turned back to Mrs. Berg. "That's for us to find out, ma'am. What killed it. Or who. That's—"

"I can't say I care for cats," said Mrs. Berg, giving a wheezy sigh. "I like their *looks*. I'm not saying they don't *look* nice. But, oh dear,

I don't like them to get too close. I'm allergic, you know."

"Aha!" said McGurk, making Mrs. Berg jump. "You getting this down, Joey?"

I looked up from my notebook and nodded. In fact, I'd already underlined the word "allergic." Twice.

"Er—is that all you wanted to know?" said Mrs. Berg. "I mean, really, it's all I can tell you. Just the feathers. I didn't actually see anything happen. I didn't even see a cat. Not even yours, Ray. But then I wasn't looking particularly."

"Well did you *hear* anything, ma'am?"

"Well. No. Nothing out of the ordinary. When do you think—?"

"Oh, early," said McGurk.

"Very early," said Wanda.

"When there usually aren't many noises at all," I said. "Even ordinary ones."

Mrs. Berg was shaking her head, her eyes nearly closed.

"No?" I said.

"No. I'm sorry. I—Oh! Just a minute!" She opened her eyes and stared over our

heads, as if listening. "I tell a lie. Now that you mention it, I *did* hear something. But it was *very* early. So early it woke me up."

We stared up at her. Waiting.

"What time would that be, ma'am?" asked McGurk, when it seemed she'd gone back into her listening trance.

"Oh . . . well . . . about half-past seven. Yes. Between seven and half-past."

We looked at one another.

It fit!

"Go on, ma'am," said McGurk. "What? What sort of noise? A fluttering?"

She shook her head slowly.

"No. Not a fluttering. More like a—well— something *metal*. A—a kind of clanging."

"A bell?"

"No. Not exactly. Duller than that. Just a dull clanging. More of a clanking, I suppose. Just two or three times, no more. Then a grunting."

"Grunting? You mean a *growling,* ma'am?"

"No. A grunting. That's duller, too. Like clanking is to clanging. That's the difference between grunting and growling. Yes, a grunting. Definitely."

Vital clues (audible)
1. A ~~clanging~~ clanking
2. A ~~grunting~~ ~~growl~~ grunting

"You got that, Joey?"

I nodded and showed him where I'd started a new page.

"I thought it might be you, Ray, doing exercises or something. Or your father just getting home from work and finding the key a bit stiff. Anyway, it soon stopped. So I turned over and went back to sleep."

That was all she could tell us. But it was a good start. We all agreed on that. Personally, I would have liked us to go somewhere quiet and discuss everything she said. I would have especially liked to talk about her and cats. About her allergy, I mean, and if she'd made any complaints about Whiskers.

But McGurk was more interested in the sounds. He couldn't wait to get back into the Williamses' yard to see if we could find a clue to that clanking and grunting.

Well, fair enough. And since Mrs. Williams still hadn't got back from the supermarket, it was a good time to go. At least we were able to concentrate on our search without her interrupting us to ask where Whiskers had gone.

So back to the feathers we went, and I must say it didn't take us long to find a clue to one of those noises.

"Look!" said Willie, standing in the narrow space between the rubbish heap and the bush. "No. Better still. Listen!"

Then he swung back his foot and gave something a kick and—sure enough—"Clunk!" that something went.

"Ow!" went Willie, almost at the same time, hopping out of the way.

"Good work, Officer Sandowsky!" said

56

McGurk. "Only you shouldn't have done it with sneakers on. Leather shoes'll give it more of a *clank*—listen."

And he too swung back his foot and gave something a kick and—sure enough—"CLANK!" that something went.

We crowded around. It was a watering can—a big old metal one. On its side, just under the bush.

"Maybe the cat knocked it over when he pounced," said Wanda.

"What cat?" said Ray, with more of a growl than a grunt.

"Too heavy," said McGurk. "Especially since it was full of water. Feel. The ground's all wet. And there's still quite a bit left inside."

"Could it have been a dog?" said Willie.

I laughed.

"Chasing *pigeons?*" I said. "Come on!"

"And what about the grunting?" said Wanda. "Growling, yes. Then I might *just* have thought about a dog. But"—she wrinkled her nose, as if the strangeness had just got to her—*"grunting. . . ?"*

"Sounds like a pig!" said Willie.

Again I laughed.

"A pigeon-hunting pig!"

"This isn't a *joke!*" growled Ray.

"No," grunted McGurk. "Cut it out. Let's carry on with the investigation. Gramp Martin next. . . . *NO!! Not that way, you dummy!*"

Willie paused, with one leg already over the low white picket fence between the Williamses' and Martins' yards.

"We want to keep him happy if we're

going to get any information," said McGurk. "So we go, nice and polite, around to his front door the proper way!"

And that's how we went to Gramp Martin. Nice and polite. The proper way.

7

Gramp Martin

Now I have already said a bit about Gramp
Martin, I know. But I had better give a few
more details, just to prepare you for the surprise we got.

First, he *looks* like a grouch. He's got plenty of hair for an old man, but it is the wiry, bushy, springy kind, and it shoots up off his head like white smoke from a hot fire. His eyebrows make him look even fiercer. They are bushy and bristly too, but still black, and they are nearly always close together in a scowl. His little eyes peer out from under them like the eyes of some small animal from a bush. A suspicious and angry small animal.

Second, he *sounds* like a grouch. He talks in quick barks and snaps. Even to other grown-ups. Even when it's only about the weather. Even to those who take pity on him and are kind to him—like Mrs. Overshaw, who cooks him a hot dinner twice a week, or Mrs. Williams, who used to be a nurse and keeps an eye on him when he's sick.

And third, there's his record. Up to about a year ago he used to have his daughter and her husband living with him. They had two kids, Jimmy and Sara. In fact, it was their house, not his. But they got so sick of him grouching at them about the garden and the house that they emigrated to Canada. That's what my father says, and I can believe him.

Anyhow, you can see why McGurk was so careful about being polite and going around there in the proper way.

And even then we felt sure we'd be told off. Just for ringing the doorbell. Just for *being* there. Only the fact that Whiskers' life was at stake made us do it, I can tell you.

So imagine it! Imagine our surprise when he took it so quietly!

"Oh, hello! What do *you* want?"

No smile, of *course*, and not exactly a warm, cheerful welcome. But for Gramp Martin it was so unusual that we wondered if he was sick.

"How—how are you, sir?" was all McGurk could think of for starters after *that* surprise.

"Fine! fine!" growled Gramp Martin. "Now what d'you want? If it's a ball you've lost, the answer's no. Certainly not. You know my rule."

This sounded more like the Gramp Martin we knew. Strangely enough, it made us feel easier. McGurk's words began to flow.

"No, nothing like that, sir. We're just investigating a mur—" McGurk checked himself. With Gramp Martin's fierce eyes on us, there was no time for fancy stuff. Anything that sounded like a game was out. Even flashing our ID cards was out. "A death," said McGurk. "A dead bird. One of the Overshaws' doves."

"Oh, yes! I did notice the feathers. Very untidy. I heard about it. What's it got to do with you?"

Ray stepped forward.

"My cat's being accused of it—that's what!" he blurted out. "Sir . . ." he added, suddenly less gruff as the fierce stare blazed down on him.

But once again, Gramp Martin cooled down. The stare stayed fierce but his voice was calm enough.

"I suppose it's only to be expected," he said. "It *is* only natural, you know, for cats to chase birds."

McGurk plucked Ray's sleeve to keep him from interrupting again.

"Yes," he said. "But not to eat the head, beak, claws, bones—everything except the

64

feathers. Not with a bird the size of a pigeon, a dove . . . sir."

But there was no need to smooth it down with another "sir." Gramp Martin stayed calm and quiet.

"Well, anyway," he said, "I'm sorry to hear about it. Very sorry."

We gaped. It looked as if the old man wasn't completely hard and mean, after all. It looked as if he had at least one soft spot. Hooray for cats, I thought—remembering how some of the wickedest tyrants in history had got soft over those creatures.

But it wasn't quite like that with Gramp Martin. His very next words proved it to be a bit different with him.

"Whatever killed that bird did me a favor," he said. "Large birds are a nuisance to gardeners like me. A real menace. It's bad enough if they're wild, but when folks are fools enough to *keep* them—grr!"

He ended with a real Grade A Gramp Martin growl.

McGurk was nodding, doing his best to look as if he too was crazy over gardening.

"I know, I know. Vermin. That's what they are really, sir."

"Public nuisances!" snarled Gramp Martin.

"Menaces!" said McGurk.

"Well?" said Gramp Martin, suddenly cocking a suspicious eye at him.

"Well, can you help with our inquiries, sir? I mean, not only do we want to clear Ray's cat—who *is* innocent. But you might like to reward the real killer. Or—er—something."

Gramp Martin gave him a long fierce stare, probably to see if he was trying to be funny.

Then he shrugged.

"There's nothing I can tell you."

"Well, did you hear anything, sir? Anything suspicious? Anything at all?"

"Not a thing. No. Nothing."

"You must have heard something," said Willie, smiling, as if we were questioning some half-wit.

Poor Willie!

He didn't know the old man as well as we did.

"I heard *nothing,* I tell you!" snarled Gramp Martin, shoving his face out at Willie.

Then, seeing us *all* back away, he simmered down. He must have made a resolution or something. Maybe his doctor had just told him he'd have to keep a hold of his temper on account of his blood pressure.

"Anyway," he said, "I think you're wasting your time. There's not much hope for the cat now. I overheard your mother, young man, and I understand it's being taken away this afternoon."

He looked so sympathetic that Ray interrupted again. This time it was a friendly interruption, not an indignant one. But from our point of view it was ten times as dangerous.

This is what he blurted out:

"No, sir. That's not true, sir. Not any more. No. We have it safe. Nothing's going to happen to Whiskers till McGurk's proved his innocence. Right, guys?"

McGurk gave him a pitying look and began shaking his head. Too late, though.

"Oh?" the old man was saying. "Is that so? You mean you've hidden it away somewhere?"

Well, by now Ray looked as if he realized

68

he'd said too much. So McGurk's head-shaking was wasted on him. The one Mc-Gurk should have been giving warnings to *now* was Willie.

"Yes!" said that boy proudly. "In our shed!"

We turned on him. Forgetting Gramp Martin and the need to be polite and orderly, we all turned on Willie.

"You dum-dum!"

"Dope!"

"Blabbermouth!"

"Idiot!"

And maybe there'd have been another round of names if Gramp Martin hadn't growled:

"That'll do!"

We turned, apologetic. But he was— well—you can hardly call it smiling. Scowling less fiercely, perhaps. With one corner of his mouth turned up.

"Don't worry," he said. "I won't give you away. I'll pretend I never heard it."

When a grouch suddenly shows he's got a decent streak after all, it can go to your head if you're not careful.

"Promise?" said McGurk.

It was a rash thing to say. It was pushing our luck terribly. And the old man's eyes blazed up.

But he really was trying. Giving his shoulders a shrug that was more of a shudder, he nodded.

"I promise," he said. "I'll not breathe a word to another living soul." Then he shook his head. "Though I don't see what good it'll do. You can't keep the cat in there forever."

"No, sir. Just till we find the right clue."

"But supposing you don't?"

"Well—well, it still might help to clear him," said McGurk, his eyes gleaming again. "Just keeping him under cover might do it."

"Oh?" said Gramp Martin, speaking just then for all of us. "How's that?"

"Well," said McGurk, grinning up at him. "If the killer strikes again. If the other dove gets killed while old Whiskers is still shut in."

The black eyebrows came together and made one bristling hedge.

"Hmm! Yes. Well. Let's hope so. . . . And now I've got to get on. I can't stand here all day talking to kids."

As we left Gramp Martin's garden, with McGurk still chirping about his latest hopeful idea, I began to feel uneasy.

"Hey, just one thing, McGurk!"

"What? What's that?"

The gleam was still there. I felt more uneasy than ever.

"You're not—you can't be—thinking of killing that other dove yourself, are you? To clear Whiskers that way? While he's shut in?"

The others gasped. But they, too, wouldn't have put it past McGurk, now that I'd mentioned it, and they all stared at him.

He looked around at us, one by one. He looked pained—deeply pained.

"If I were an ordinary citizen I might. Yes. Sure. If it were my cat I might think of it. Yes. Sure. But when the McGurk Organization has to solve a mystery by *cheating*, that's when we tear up our ID cards."

"Sorry, McGurk!" I said.

And meant it.

But I got to thinking about that conversation before another twenty-four hours had passed.

About the second victim theory, I mean.

I got to thinking about it hard, trying to remember just what had been said, and how loud.

8

Shock Number One

At first, though, we had other problems.

Ray, for instance, had to explain to his mother that the cat had escaped. He had to explain that he had opened the door and that Whiskers had gone through. This was true enough in a way, of course. But it didn't matter. She believed that he had deliberately let Whiskers go. She made Ray go look for him, but—as Ray had guessed—she wasn't all that bothered when he returned without the cat.

"All she hopes is that he won't come back of his own accord," Ray said. "Just so long as she's rid of him. Just so long as the neighbors don't have anything else to complain about."

"Why is she so worried about the neighbors?" I asked.

"It's because my father works nights and sleeps days. She's afraid that if we cause any trouble to the neighbors, the neighbors'll start getting back at us by making loud noises. Playing radios in the yard. That sort of thing. So my father won't be able to sleep."

The reason I got to talk so much with Ray was because of another of our problems. Mc-Gurk had put Willie and me on special duty for the rest of that day. To keep an eye on Willie's shed at all times.

"Make sure nobody goes in there," Mc-Gurk said. "Head them off if they try. You,

Willie—if your father or mother look like they're going in there for something, offer to get it yourself. Pretend you're on a good behavior campaign. Trying for an increase in your allowance. Or throw a fit. Get Joey to clip you one and have a nosebleed. Anything. *Only don't let them go in and find Whiskers!*"

And the reason why I'd been sent with Willie on this mission was because I live next door.

"That means you can do some of the staking out from Joey's yard," McGurk explained. "So it doesn't look too obvious. So they won't start wondering why you're hanging around in *their* yard all the time."

Then McGurk had added one more thing: one extra duty.

Lowering his voice, he said:

"And, hey—Joey, Willie. Keep an eye on Ray, too. If I know him he'll be around every five minutes wanting to look at Whiskers. Stop him. Or at least ration him. One peek every two hours. Otherwise he'll attract attention to the shed. And *that* we do not want." It made sense.

For McGurk was dead right about Ray. The way that boy fussed about his cat, you'd have thought it was his *son* or something. The funny thing was, though, that Whiskers couldn't have cared less. We let Ray smuggle in another can of cat food early in the afternoon. After Whiskers had dug into that, he went straight to his sacks, curled up, and went to sleep! As happy as if he'd lived there all his life!

Anyway, there we were—Willie and I— stuck with the job of keeping one eye on the shed and another on Ray.

Meanwhile, the rest of the Organization were having their own problems.

All further investigations they made drew a big fat zero.

They found no more clues.

Nobody they spoke to had heard or seen a thing.

Perhaps if I'd been going around with them, with my notebook and my keen eyes (don't be fooled by the glasses!), I might have spotted something.

Perhaps if Willie had been going around with them, with his keen nose, he might have sniffed out something.

But I doubt it.

I mean, McGurk and Wanda took long enough. Hours, they spent. Dozens of people, they questioned. And what had they to show for it?

Nothing.

Wanda looked fed up when she and Mc-Gurk came over to our stakeout that evening. But McGurk—well, McGurk's McGurk. Ever hopeful.

"Tomorrow's another day," he said. "And I say we begin early. Seven o'clock A.M."

"*So* early?" I said.

"On a *Sunday?*" protested Willie.

"Yes. Why not? It was *so* early when the murder took place, wasn't it? There must be all sorts of people who are around at that time. People we haven't questioned yet. *Early-morning* people."

"All sorts?"

"Well . . . you know. . . . People who wake early and take their dogs walking. . . . People coming home from night work. . . . Newspaper boys."

We had to admit that again it made sense.

"And listen," said McGurk. "Instead of meeting at Headquarters, we'll start out right here in your yard, Joey. It's nearer the scene of the crime and—"

"Yes!" said Ray. "And Whiskers will be ready for an early-morning saucer of milk."

"So that settles it," said McGurk, still looking at me and Willie and Wanda. "Seven sharp. Here. . . ." Then he turned to Ray. "One thing," he said. "Do *not* come around with a carton of milk in your hand. That *would* attract attention."

"But—"

"Let Willie do it," said McGurk. "He's

only got a few steps to go. Down his own yard."

"All right," said Ray. Then he gave Willie a fierce look. "But you'd better make sure it's a fresh carton! He can't stand it even if it's only a *day* old."

And that's how we came to be in my back yard, behind the garage, at seven the next morning, when the two shocks arrived.

"Hey!" gasped Ray Williams, running up with the first of them. "Listen! It's *happened!*"

We stared.

"What?" said McGurk. *"What's* happened?"

"Another! There's been another! Another murder! Same place exactly!"

Shock Number Two

When this took place, there was just Wanda, McGurk and me, besides Ray.

Willie was a bit late.

In fact it wasn't until Ray had come running up that Willie had shown his nose. I happened to see him out of the corner of my eye, coming out of his back door, carrying a saucer of milk, and starting out furtively for the shed.

But of course, Ray's news made us forget about Willie right away.

"Well, that's it, men!" McGurk was saying. His already shining morning face was shining even brighter. "That's just what I said might happen. It clears our client completely."

He looked as pleased as Ray—and that boy was delighted. I didn't think the news was all that bad, either. Only Wanda looked a bit sad.

"Poor thing!" she said. "The day after its brother was killed, too!"

"No, you've got it wrong," said Ray. "It wasn't the other *dove*. It was just an ordinary pigeon this time. One of those blue-gray ones. But it was in exactly the same place, near the rubbish heap. And it proves exactly the same thing. Huh, McGurk? It proves—"

"That our client isn't the killer," said McGurk. "Yes. Just like I said. Now we've only got to—"

And there he stopped.

Because that's when the second shock arrived.

This time it was Willie who ran up.

Willie with his eyes staring and his nose red and his face white. Willie with milk spilled all down the front of his shirt.

"Hey!"

"Good heavens, Willie! What's the matter?"

He didn't seem to hear Wanda.

He just stood gazing at us, from face to face, saying "Hey!" to each one.

"What is it?"

McGurk was sounding annoyed.

"I—have any of you—I mean—hey!—is this a joke?"

"Is *what* a joke?" growled Ray, suddenly going white himself as he stared at the milk stains.

"The cat!" said Willie. "I—I'm not kidding. It—it's gone! Vanished! Disappeared!"

10
The Mystery of the Closed But Open Door

The first thing we did was go search the shed. Not for clues, but for the cat itself.

"He may be hiding in a corner," said McGurk, as we approached the shed.

"He'd better be!" said Ray, scowling at Willie.

"I looked! Honest!"

"You couldn't have been very thorough," said Wanda. "There's so much junk in there."

"But I—"

"Shut up!" said McGurk. "This isn't doing any good. Willie—go get a flashlight, and be quick about it. You others wait. We don't go in there until we have a better light."

Willie was glad to get out of Ray's reach.

When he returned, McGurk took the flashlight from him and said:

"Right. Just in case the cat *is* in there—"

"But that's—" began Willie.

"He's just *got* to be in there!" said Ray.

"All right! All right!" said McGurk. "What I'm saying is this. Be careful when you go in, so he doesn't slip out between our legs."

We were careful. Very careful. And as soon as we were inside, we shut the door.

"Aw, look!" said Wanda, as the light shone on the box of soil. "See how tidily he's used his litter box."

"Never mind that!" said McGurk. "Start looking."

But it was no use.

We looked behind boxes. We looked behind rusty spades and some old pictures leaning against the walls. We looked under a stack of broken garden chairs. We even looked *inside* the sacks on the pile on the shelf, although Whiskers would have had to be a very flat cat to be there, so well pressed down had he made them.

"So how did he get out?" I said. "I know some cats can push down on old-fashioned catches and open the door for themselves. But this is a door*knob*. Whiskers couldn't possibly have opened this."

"Well—" began Willie, but again he was too slow.

"Holes. Loose boards," said McGurk. "Rips in the roof. Start looking. Anything like that."

So we did. We looked at every inch of every inside surface of that shed. More than once. Some of us systematically, a bit at a time, like Wanda and me. Others darting here and there, like Willie and Ray. And others—well, *one* other—picking all the likeliest places for himself.

And we didn't just look, either. We prodded and probed and pried, testing for loose places. We squeezed fingers into cracks and tugged. We thumped upward at the roof, especially in the corners, and sent spiders shuttling for safety.

But no chink or crack, no slit or slot, no gap or rip or crevice or cavity that we found was wide enough for a rat to squeeze through or in, let alone a big, fine cat. That shed may have been old and dirty and neglected, but it was solid.

Which left only one thing.

We all seemed to think of it at once.

"All right, Willie," said McGurk. "Tell us what happened. Exactly."

We all turned and stared at Willie. McGurk shined the light on his face. He blinked.

"Well—well I've been *trying* to, haven't I? But, well—the door *was* open, you know."

"Open?!!"

I think we *all* repeated that word.

Then Ray went on:

"So it *is* your fault! You dummy! You left it—"

"No, no! I shut it. Cross my heart. The last time we looked in. Just after eight last night. I mean *he* was with me. Weren't you? Didn't I? *You* tell them!"

I nodded. It was true. Willie by himself might have made a mistake like that. But me—never.

"Firmly shut," I said. "I tested it myself."

The others were looking mystified now. Willie seemed to take courage.

"Yet just now," he said, "when I went with the milk, it was open. Well, shut really. But open. If you see what I mean."

Ray howled.

"Shut but open! This kid's a fool!"

But McGurk was more thoughtful. He shook his head and said quietly:

"No. We don't see what you mean, Willie."

"Well, come on out and I'll show you."

We trooped out.

Then Willie pushed the door until it was closed, except for the catch itself. I mean there was no gap, but the catch wasn't actually fast in place.

91

"Closed, you see," said Willie. "But open."

We all nodded. Even so, I was the first to notice the really odd thing.

"Hey!" I said. "This means that even if we had left the door open, or the catch unfastened, which we didn't—well, it means that the cat could have pushed his way out all right—yes—but—"

"Exactly!" said Ray. "Of course he can push a door open if the catch isn't fastened. And that's what *must* have happened, you dummies!"

"No, no. Let me finish," I said. "Because if that *had* happened, Whiskers must have been very polite. Very polite indeed. *Fantastically* polite, even for a cat."

"What do you mean?"

"I know!" said McGurk. "He means Whiskers would have had to turn around and try to shut the door. Like a person. Good thinking, Officer Rockaway."

"Hmm!" murmured Wanda. "I suppose the wind could have done it. Blown it shut."

"What wind?" I said. "There's been no wind lately. Besides—feel." I prodded the door on its stiff, rusty hinges. "It would have

taken a gale," I said, only getting it shut with quite a bit of force.

Wanda nodded, satisfied.

"All I can think of," said McGurk, "is that some snooper, some prowler, must have opened it in the night. Someone looking for something to steal. Then he shut it again, or thought he had, when he saw there was nothing worth taking."

"Yes," I said. "And with Whiskers slipping out between *his* legs, while he was snooping."

"Anyway," said Ray, "that's not the point now. The point is that Whiskers has gone. The point is that he *hasn't* been shut up in here all the time. And you know what that means."

He was looking very upset again.

"Yes," I said. "It means that his alibi's blown. For the second murder."

Suddenly McGurk snapped his fingers.

"Ah, yes! That! I'd forgotten. There's *that!* . . . Come on, men. Let's examine the body. You never know. We might find some real clues this time."

"What about Whiskers?" said Ray.

"He won't have gone far," said McGurk. "Cats never do."

He was moving out into the street already.

"No," murmured Wanda, as we followed him, with Ray a few steps behind us. "I'm afraid he's right. Cats never do stray far. Rarely, anyway."

"What do you mean—*afraid?*"

"Keep your voice down," she said, glancing back at Ray. "It's just that I can't help feeling that Whiskers himself might be the *real clue* we find. If you see what I'm getting at."

I nodded glumly.

I did see.

Only too well!

11

Framed?

There was no need to draw a plan of the Williamses' yard this time. The remains were scattered very much in the same pattern: bunching around the corner near the garbage heap, then thinning out.

But there were important differences that had nothing to do with the pattern. Two important differences, to be exact. And the first thing I did was note them down:

Murder No. 2
[Place]: same
[Time]: sometime before 7:30 A.M.
N.B. 2 Important Differences:
1. Type of feathers — ordinary blue-gray pigeon feathers
2. Remains = more than just feathers. Includes head, claws, one complete wing, bones

Ray had already told us about Difference No. 1, of course. So I should have been able to concentrate on noting down all the different parts of the pigeon besides feathers. I mean *exactly*. Not simply mentioning "head, claws, one complete wing, bones"—the way I wrote it down.

But there wasn't time.

McGurk was yelling at everybody to stand back and give me a chance to make my notes properly, when Mrs. Williams came out of the house. She was in her bathrobe and her hair was still in curlers. It was a blood-red bathrobe, and the curlers were metal ones that flashed in the morning sun, and somehow she didn't look timid any more.

"Well," she said, "that does it!"

"But, Mom," Ray began, "how do we know it was—?"

"Same place. Same mess. Same time. Two days running."

"But Whiskers isn't *here*, Mom. He's gone off. He's gone—"

"He's gone *wild*, more like it!" said Mrs. Williams. "He's gone back to the wild state. He's gone into hiding, but he's still around. I distinctly heard him miaowing during the night. I thought it might be some other cat, but—"

"Well, it might have been, ma'am," said McGurk politely. "And it might have been some other cat that did this, too."

She blinked at him snappily.

"Well, I'm glad to know you're starting to see sense, young man. The last I heard of you and your theories, you were saying cats don't eat birds this size."

"I *still* say that, ma'am. Not the *whole* bird, bones and all. But look—there's more than half this bird left. So it could have been a cat this time. And—"

"And it *was* a cat!" said Mrs. Williams grimly. "And here *is* that cat now!"

She was looking over our heads toward the side of the yard next to the Bergs.

We all turned.

"Whiskers!" gasped Ray.

Sure enough, there was our client, just squeezing through the railings.

We were all stunned. Even Wanda and I, who had been half afraid that Whiskers himself would turn out to be the vital clue at the scene of *this* crime.

We were so stunned that we didn't do anything but stand there gaping for a few

seconds. During this time, the cat came toward us slowly, casually, calmly. He paused to sniff at a flower, then continued to advance, with his tail high in the air.

When he reached the first feathers, he stopped to sniff at them, too. But he didn't waste much time on them. He seemed far too interested in the group that was standing watching him. So he gave a soft chirp and covered the last few yards in a little bounding run. Then he flopped on the grass at Ray's feet and rolled over on his back.

"That cat's far too sweet to be a murderer!" said Wanda quietly.

Her voice broke the spell.

"GRAB HIM!" yelled McGurk.

He made some of us jump.

"That was the idea!" he told us afterward. "I could see Mrs. Williams was going to pick Whiskers up. So I yelled like that hoping to scare him off. I didn't really *mean* for anyone to grab him."

Well, it almost worked.

Mrs. Williams was one of those who jumped, and it made her jerk her arms about just as she was reaching out for the cat.

And Whiskers himself jumped. He stopped rolling on his back, twisted round onto his feet, and looked all set to run away for real.

Then Willie grabbed him. Yes—Willie. Good old Willie.

The Head of the Organization had yelled "Grab him!" and Officer Sandowsky had grabbed.

"If I'd *meant* it," McGurk complained afterward, "if I'd really wanted that cat caught, if our lives had depended on it— you'd have *missed!*"

But Willie didn't. He even managed to hang on to the startled, wriggling animal.

Then:

"Thank you!" said Mrs. Williams, taking Whiskers from him and holding the cat close to her bathrobe. "I'm glad to see one of you has some sense. Now—"

"Aw, Mom!"

Ray sounded like he was just about to cry.

"Now it comes into the house with me. And stays there until your father gets up. It will be treated kindly—don't worry. But this time there will be no mistake. No accident. All right?"

The cat had relaxed at the sound of her voice. He was snuggling closer and squeezing his eyes again. His front paws hung limply over her arm. He let himself be carried into the house like a lamb.

A lamb to the slaughter.

"That woman," said Wanda softly, "doesn't *deserve*—"

I nudged her.

"It's Ray's mother you're talking about, remember."

"Ha! You can say what you like about her!" cried Ray. "She's nothing but a—"

"Be quiet a minute!"

McGurk's voice sounded so urgent that Ray broke off and we all turned to look.

McGurk was on one knee, on the grass, among the feathers and other remains. He was holding the dead bird's feet up by the claws, dangling them in front of his eyes.

"The cat," he murmured, still staring at the claws. "Nearly human, isn't he? The way he listens. The way he talks. . . ."

"What does that matter *now*?" said Ray bitterly.

The tears had already started running down his cheeks.

"But I'll tell you what," said McGurk, with a peculiar smile. "I bet he's not so human that he eats with a knife and fork. Eh? I bet he's not all *that* human!"

"McGurk!" gasped Wanda. "Cut the joking! Can't you see Ray's awfully upset?"

The smile went from McGurk's face. He stood up.

"I am *not* joking!" he said. "Because look. How come the claws have been cut off clean? With a knife? Just like a chicken at a supermarket?"

We crowded closer. Even Ray wiped away his tears to get a better look.

And McGurk was right.

Those claws *had* been cut.

"But—what's it *mean?*" whispered Willie.

"It means," said McGurk, "that this murder was not done by a cat, or a dog, or a pig. It means that this murder—and the other one, too, I'll bet you—these murders were done by a *human*. It means that Whiskers has been *framed!*"

12
The New Clue

"Framed?" said Willie. "What's that mean?"

McGurk was carefully wrapping the claws in his handkerchief.

"It means that someone has deliberately made it look like a cat's crime. So that Whiskers will get the blame. That's what framing means. Someone has tried to frame him. And these claws prove it." He put them in his shirt pocket and patted it. "Exhibit A," he said. "Proof."

"Yes, but *who?*" said Wanda.

"Yeah!" growled Ray. "That's what I'd like to know. And when I do—"

"When you do will be *never!"* said Mc-Gurk. "If we stand here yacking all morning. Come on. We've got to take another look around Willie's shed. This time for clues. Because whoever let that cat out is the one who's been trying to frame him."

He was walking away quickly as he was saying all this. Ray was up front with him, nearly tripping over his own feet in his hurry. I suppose he was more aware than any of us that Whiskers had only an hour or two left to live if we didn't find the real killer soon. I suppose in poor Ray's mind he kept seeing his father and mother, imagining what they were doing, how close his father was to getting up, getting washed and shaved, getting dressed, getting his breakfast, getting the car out, getting Whiskers into the car. . . .

But my own mind was freer to think carefully. To try to work out just who it might
have been who'd tried to frame Whiskers.

"Could it be Mrs. Williams herself?" I said
to Wanda and Willie as we hurried along.

"I wouldn't put it past her," said Wanda.
"She's certainly in a rush to get rid of him."

"Yes," said Willie, "but only because she
thinks he *is* the killer."

I nodded. For once, Willie seemed to be
right. Still, you never knew. I wasn't crossing
Mrs. Williams off altogether.

"Then again, it could be Mrs. Berg," I
said.

"Oh?" said Willie. "Why?"

"I know," said Wanda.

"Go on, then," I said. "Why?"

"Because she's allergic to cats. Because they
make her asthma bad. She said so herself.
And Whiskers does live next door."

Again I nodded. To my mind, Mrs. Berg
was a stronger suspect than Mrs. Williams.
Yet even so, she wasn't what McGurk would
call a *prime* suspect. After all, she'd never
complained about the cat, not even when
she was telling us about her allergy. And as

far as I knew it was only when people like her were shut in the same room as a cat that they were in any danger.

"What about Ray himself?" said Wanda. "Have you thought about *that?*"

This came as such a shock that I stopped and Willie stumbled into me.

"Ray? Framing his own *cat?*"

"Keep your voice down. . . . Yes. Ray."

"But—"

"I don't mean he'd be trying to get the cat *into* trouble, though," Wanda continued. "More likely trying to get him *out* of it."

"What's she talking about?" said Willie.

"Don't ask *me!*" I said.

"And I thought you were the one with brains!" jeered Wanda. "Listen. What I mean is that Ray could have killed that second pigeon himself. Somehow. Then chopped it up to make it look as if a cat had done it. Not knowing that someone had let Whiskers out. Thinking it would clear Whiskers' name."

"Hmm! Well. Yes. I suppose so."

I suddenly remembered what McGurk had said when I'd suggested that *he* might try something like that: "If I was an ordinary

citizen, I might. . . . If it was *my* cat, I might. . . ."

Well, it was *Ray's* cat, wasn't it?

Suppose what McGurk had said had given him the idea?

But then I shook my head.

Ray was too eager to get back to Willie's shed to search for clues. If he'd chopped that pigeon up he would have known that such a search would be hopeless. He wouldn't have been up there, ahead of McGurk himself. He might even have stayed behind. Hoping to get his mother to change her mind. Or hoping to talk his father out of it. Or hoping to release the cat again.

But no.

"Hey! Come on, you guys!" he was yelling now, at Willie's front gate. "My cat's life depends on this! Get a move on!"

We got a move on.

McGurk took charge.

"Willie—get your flashlight again. You and I are going to look inside. . . . Ray, you search the ground at the front of the shed, starting at the door and working out. . . . Joey, this side, from the wall out. . . . Wanda, the other side, same system. . . . Me, I'll just have a look around the back while I'm waiting for Willie."

"But what are we looking for?" asked Wanda.

"A clue," said McGurk. "What do you think?"

"Yes, but—"

"Anything the person who came around here last night might have dropped," said McGurk. "A cigarette butt, a—a glove, a—well—a handkerchief with his initials on it. *You* know."

"Oh, sure!" said Wanda. "Why not a calling card? Complete with his address and telephone number?"

But even as she was making this crack, she was busy looking. We all were. Maybe, like me, the others had just had a picture in their minds of Mr. Williams putting his shirt on and saying: "Don't bother with breakfast. I don't feel like any. I'll just run the cat around to the pound first. . . ."

It was Ray himself who found the clue.

Willie and McGurk were busy inside the hut, and Wanda and I had worked our way a couple of yards back from the sides, when suddenly there was a yell:

"Hey! How about *this?*"

Ray was holding up something, close to the door. McGurk nearly knocked him over as he came bursting out.

"What? What? What have you got, Ray?"

"This—this candy wrapper. I missed it the first time around. Someone had tromped it into the grass. But it looks somehow *new* to me—you know—*recent.* Doesn't it?"

It was a small scrap of waxed paper— grayish white with red lettering. It was damp, and not very clean, yet we had to agree that it did look new. Something to do with its springiness, and the clearness of the printing. When you pick up three pailsful of litter, like we had the day before, you get to know the look and feel of *old* candy wrappers. They look faded. They feel limp.

"Hand it over," said McGurk.

He smoothed it out.

We inspected it.

Here it is—Exhibit B in the Case of the Condemned Cat:

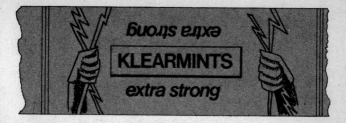

"Ugh!" said Wanda. "I hate them. They're so strong they burn my tongue."

"Mine, too," said Willie.

"So it's not one of yours?" said McGurk.

"No, *sir!*" said Willie. "Not sweet enough, either. Besides, they're so strong they'd ruin my sensitive sense of smell."

"Never mind your nose!" said McGurk. "We want to know who might have dropped this. What about your mother or father?"

"Nah!" said Willie, very definitely. "Never touch them. Now if my grandfather had ever been to this house, I'd have said it was his. He *loves* them. So did my grandmother when she was alive. It's a real old people's kind of candy. It—"

"Hold it!"

McGurk's eyes were gleaming as he looked around at us.

"Has anyone ever noticed anyone around here unwrapping one?"

We frowned as we tried to think. Ray was nibbling his lip. Wanda was scowling up at a cloud. Willie had closed his eyes.

Then suddenly he opened them.

"Well, not exactly," he said. "But like I say, it's mainly old folks. Gramp Martin, for instance. Now I've never seen him *un-wrapping* one, but . . . well . . ."

"Go on, go on! But what?"

"Er—permission to speak about my nose, sir?" said Willie, with a sheepish grin.

"Go *on!*" snarled Ray. "Or I promise you, I'll *flatten* it!"

"Well," said Willie, backing off and looking serious. "Yesterday. When Gramp Martin yelled at me and stuck his face out. Well—*then*—then I could smell this very sort of mint on his breath!"

"Gramp Martin!" murmured McGurk.

"Next door to us!" said Ray.

"The only one apart from us who knew where Whiskers was hidden!" said Wanda.

"And of *course!*" I cried. "To a gardening nut like him, cats are just as big a menace as pigeons. Why, this way he could kill two birds with one stone!"

"One cat with two birds, you mean," said Wanda. "The horrid old man!"

"What are we waiting for?" said Ray grimly.

13

Showdown

On the way over to Gramp Martin's, McGurk
gave his usual warning.

"Leave everything to me. Understand? *All*
the talking."

But this time he said it so firmly that I

could see it wasn't just because he was being bossy. There was really no need for him to add:

"I have an idea."

Nobody argued. The only one who said anything was Ray.

"Well, I hope it's a good one. What is it?"

"No time to explain," said McGurk. "We've got to get him to confess and clear Whiskers before— Well. You know."

Ray gulped. He knew, all right. We all knew. We didn't want to waste even a second.

All we hoped was that McGurk's idea would match the gleam in his eyes.

If it didn't, that would be the end of Whiskers.

Anyway, we were soon filing down Gramp Martin's path, ringing the bell, standing behind McGurk.

I noticed McGurk's fingers were crossed.

Gramp Martin wasn't so easy to deal with this time. He was more like his usual self.

"Go away!" he snarled, as soon as he opened the door. "This is getting to be a nuisance!"

His eyebrows were clumped together again. His little eyes peered angrily at us.

"Sorry, sir," said McGurk. "But—"

"I didn't see or hear anything *this* time, either," snapped the old man. "All right?"

I thought he was going to slam the door there and then. But McGurk took a step forward and said, almost as sharply:

"What do you mean? *This* time?"

No "sir," notice.

That pulled Gramp Martin up. He looked furious, but he was forced to answer.

"The pigeon," he said. "This morning."

McGurk became polite again. But also sly—leering a bit.

"How do you know about that, sir? We hadn't mentioned it."

The old man snorted. McGurk was really getting under his skin.

"I can *see,* can't I? I've only to look over my fence to see another untidy mess! Now clear off. I—"

"Anyway, sir, it's not *that* that we've come for. It's something much more serious. It's about who came to Willie's shed last night and let Whiskers out."

The old man opened his mouth, then shut it again. The angry look left his eyes. They became shifty, then cautious, then crafty. This time when he spoke he had to force himself to snap. I could tell.

"How should I know anything about that? It's way at the other end of the street."

Before McGurk could stop her, Wanda blurted out:

"You were the only one who knew the cat was in there besides us!"

Now Gramp Martin looked really mad.

"Are you accusing *me* of—?"

But he didn't get any further, because that's when McGurk put his idea into action. Already he'd taken out the mint wrapper. He was fiddling with it, seemingly nervous, not knowing what he was doing. Just smoothing it out, then twisting it and untwisting it. And crossing and uncrossing his fingers at the same time.

The old man didn't take any notice of this at first. It was McGurk's words that had pulled him up.

"Of course we're not accusing you, Mr.

Martin. It's just that it's a very serious crime and the police will be coming around later."

Gramp Martin relaxed a bit.

"Serious crime?" he said, sneering. *"Police* coming? . . . What? To find out who let a cat out of a shed?"

McGurk shook his head.

"No. Not that. That was just accidental, sir. But a valuable electric lawn-mower was stolen out of the shed last night."

Next to me, Willie gasped. I gave him a sharp nudge to keep him quiet. I didn't know what McGurk was getting at myself just then, but I could see it was having an effect on Gramp Martin. He was gaping now—not knowing what to say. And he was finding it very hard not to look at the mint wrapper that McGurk was fiddling with.

"So that's why the police have been called," said McGurk. "They're going to send someone around to look for fingerprints and they've told Mr. Sandowsky to keep us away from the shed." McGurk sighed. I think he really meant it when he added: "I wish *we* could take fingerprints. . . ."

"But—but—why—"

It was no good. Gramp Martin was just speechless. McGurk waited politely, then went on:

"They're going to talk to Joey's mother, too."

I didn't gasp. I was beginning to see what McGurk was trying to do. So I backed him up and crossed my own fingers and nodded my head. Gramp Martin gave a little shudder as his eyes flitted back to McGurk.

"His—mother? Mrs.—Rockaway?"

McGurk nodded.

"Next door to the Sandowskys. She says she saw someone sneaking into the yard late last night. She says she recognized him. She says it was someone who lives around here. She says she didn't think much of it at the time, because it was someone respectable. Or that's what she'd always thought. A very respectable person, she said. She thought he was just borrowing something. Some gardening tools or something."

"Did—did she say—?"

McGurk shook his head and sighed again.

"She wouldn't tell *us* who it was."

Gramp Martin seemed to relax a bit. Then he jumped when McGurk reminded him:

"She'll only tell the real police, when they come to take her statement. So we're trying to *show* them. We're trying to solve the case before the real police arrive. And we were wondering—"

But Gramp Martin wasn't listening any more. Gramp Martin's hands were shaking. Gramp Martin was in a panic the way poor Ray had been in a panic.

"But—but I only opened the door," he croaked. "I didn't even go *in!*"

McGurk pretended to be shocked.

"*You*, sir?"

Gramp Martin's eyebrows came back together.

"Yes! *Me*, you little fool! Me! I—all right! I *did* go to let the cat out. You were right, young lady, when you said I was the only one who knew you'd hidden it there. You all told me. So be sure you remember that, when the police ask. Because that's all I *did* do. Understand? Let the cat out. There's no crime in that, is there?"

"Isn't there?" cried Ray. "What about—?"

McGurk grabbed his arm and pulled him back.

This time he pretended to be puzzled.

"But I don't get it, sir. *Why* did you let the cat out?"

"Because . . ." Suddenly Gramp Martin's shoulders slumped and his face went sort of flabby. "Oh, well . . . look . . . I—I'm sorry. It was an accident. It all started with an accident, when—"

"Just a minute, sir." McGurk held up a hand. His fingers were no longer crossed. He looked very pleased with himself. "You getting this down, Joey?"

I nodded. My notebook was already turned to a new page. I had already started the heading that was later to be typed for the records:

```
CONFESSION

- made in the presence of:
J. McGurk
J. Rockaway
W. Sandowsky
W. Grieg, and
R. Williams (representing the
        client, W. Williams).
```

"Go on, sir," said McGurk quietly.

Then the old man confessed. In full. And it was a true confession. We knew that because it checked out with all the facts and every clue.

14

Confession

It had all started the day before. Not long after dawn.

"It was a beautiful morning and I was up early, as usual," said Gramp Martin. "I was out in the garden. Working. While everybody else was asleep in their beds—you included."

He gave us a glare, as if he was about to start on a lecture about how lazy young people were these days. Then he must have remembered how busy we five had been. So he sighed and got on with his confession.

"I was lifting some new plants out of their pots, ready to bed out. Then, out of the corner of my eye, I saw one of those pesky white doves. Swooping down as if it lived here. Right onto my young strawberries."

Usually he'd kept a net over the strawberries. But because he was going to be putting the new plants into the bed next to them, he had drawn the net aside.

"Well, when I saw it digging away at the beautiful new fruits—best crop I ever had—I lost my temper, and—bang!—I threw a plant pot at it. The one I had in my hand. Still loaded with damp earth and pretty heavy." He looked at us with the thick eyebrows raised and his eyes wider than we'd ever seen them. "Truly," he said, "really and truly, I never expected to *hit* the bird."

McGurk, Ray, Willie, and I nodded. *We* knew about throwing things at moving targets. We believed him.

Wanda wasn't so sure.

"I should hope *not!*"

Gramp Martin gave her a sour stare.

"Anyway. That's what happened. When I went up to it, there it was. Stone dead. So then—well—I got worried."

What I think he meant was that he panicked. He probably thought about the hot dinners Mrs. Overshaw made for him, and how they might stop now because of this.

"At first I thought of burying it as it was. Luckily, no one was around to see me. And then I had a better idea. Before burying it, why not pluck the feathers off, strew them around, and make it look as if a cat had done it? Then Mrs. Overshaw wouldn't be in suspense. Wondering if it would come back. Worrying."

"Very thoughtful!" said Ray bitterly. "What about *us* being in suspense? Worrying about the cat?"

Gramp Martin didn't say anything to that except: "Anyway, that's what I did. I took the feathers to the fence, stepped over, and—"

"Stumbled into a watering can and grunted with surprise," murmured McGurk, his eyes gleaming. "Right?"

Gramp Martin grunted with surprise again.

"Why, yes! How did—?" Then he shrugged. "What does it matter? It's over now. I'll go straight to Mrs. Williams and explain."

"No. Wait a minute," said McGurk, looking across to the Williamses' garage to make sure the car hadn't been brought out yet. "What about later, sir? The pigeon. Did you kill that?"

"Certainly not!" snapped Gramp Martin. "I told you the first one was an accident. I don't go around killing pigeons, nuisances though they are. No. What happened there, was . . ."

And he told us how worried he'd been when we came around investigating. Especially when McGurk had mentioned there were no bones or claws, or anything. He could see that people might begin to suspect the dove had been killed by a human after all.

"So this time I had to make *sure* it looked like a cat. So I went to the meat and poultry market and bought an unplucked pigeon there. And I cut it up and—and—"

"And let Whiskers out, yes!" said Ray. "And that's what I can't understand. At least you could have left him there and made it look as if *another* cat had done this second killing. But no!"

"Yes, well ... I'm sorry," said Gramp Martin. "But there it is. I—I just didn't think. I mean I thought your parents would just try to keep the cat in your own yard more. Maybe in the house. Keep it more under control. . . ."

So we had been right. The old grouch had seen his way to tackling another of his enemies at the same time. That was all hogwash about thinking the cat would be kept indoors instead of being put to sleep. Hadn't he said in that first interview that he'd overheard Mrs. Williams talking about sending the cat to the pound? He'd framed Whiskers, all right.

A sound from over the fence made us turn that way. Mr. Williams was opening the garage doors.

"You'd better go and tell my father all this, hadn't you?" said Ray. "Right now. Before it's too late."

And to give him his due, Gramp Martin did just that. It must have been hard, but I suppose it was all he could do. And whether he stuck to his story about not expecting Whiskers to be condemned to death for the "crime" we don't know. The main thing was that our client was cleared.

The car was left in the garage. Mrs. Williams herself lifted Whiskers out of the basket they'd put him in, and she hugged him, and walked around the garden still hugging him, saying she was sorry, until he struggled out of her arms and came across to thank his *real* friends—who'd never doubted him a single minute—with his tail high in the air.

And that was that.

As for Gramp Martin—well—he did look a bit mad when he found out that nothing had been stolen from the shed after all. But I think he was relieved, too, at being able to get it off his chest. Of course, he was very careful to smooth things over with his neighbors on the other side. Not only did he buy the Overshaws another dove, he also built them a dovecote.

"You could almost say it's made him a bird lover," said Wanda, when we heard about this.

"Well, a bird *tolerator*," I corrected her.

"Cats and kids he still doesn't care for, though," said Willie. "Ray says he still gets mad when he sees Whiskers in his garden. And you should have heard him when I went to ask for my Frisbee back!"

"Well, that's his privilege," said McGurk. "We set out to save Whiskers' life, not to make a new man out of Gramp Martin."

Then his face clouded a bit.

"There's only one thing that spoils that case, though."

"What?"

"Well, since it was an accident, him killing that dove, it doesn't actually rate as murder."

"No," I said. "I've already changed it in the records. To manslaughter."

"How about *bird*slaughter?" said Wanda, trying to be clever.

But surprisingly enough it was Willie who had the last word this time. Sighing happily, he said:

"Just so long as it wasn't *cat*slaughter!"

ABOUT THE AUTHOR

E. W. Hildick has written over forty children's books. Archway Paperback editions include **A Cat Called Amnesia, The Top-Flight, Fully-Automated Junior High School Girl Detective,** and the **McGurk Mystery** series, which now has six titles: **Deadline for McGurk, The Case of the Condemned Cat, The Case of the Nervous Newsboy, The Great Rabbit Rip-Off, The Case of the Invisible Dog,** and **The Case of the Secret Scribbler.** Mr. Hildick's books have been published in over a dozen countries. A British subject, he and his wife divide their time between homes in England and the United States.

ABOUT THE ILLUSTRATOR

Lisl Weil, who has been writing and illustrating for many years, has over eighty children's books to her credit. Each year Ms. Weil performs at Young People's Concerts with major symphony orchestras, illustrating a story in the rhythm of the music. She lives in New York City.